This igloo book belongs to:

....

igloobooks

Published in 2016
by Igloo Books Ltd
Cottage Farm
Sywell
NN6 0BJ
www.igloobooks.com

LEO002 0116
2 4 6 8 10 9 7 5 3 1
ISBN: 978-1-78557-653-9

Written by Melanie Joyce
Illustrated by Daniel Howarth

Printed and manufactured in China

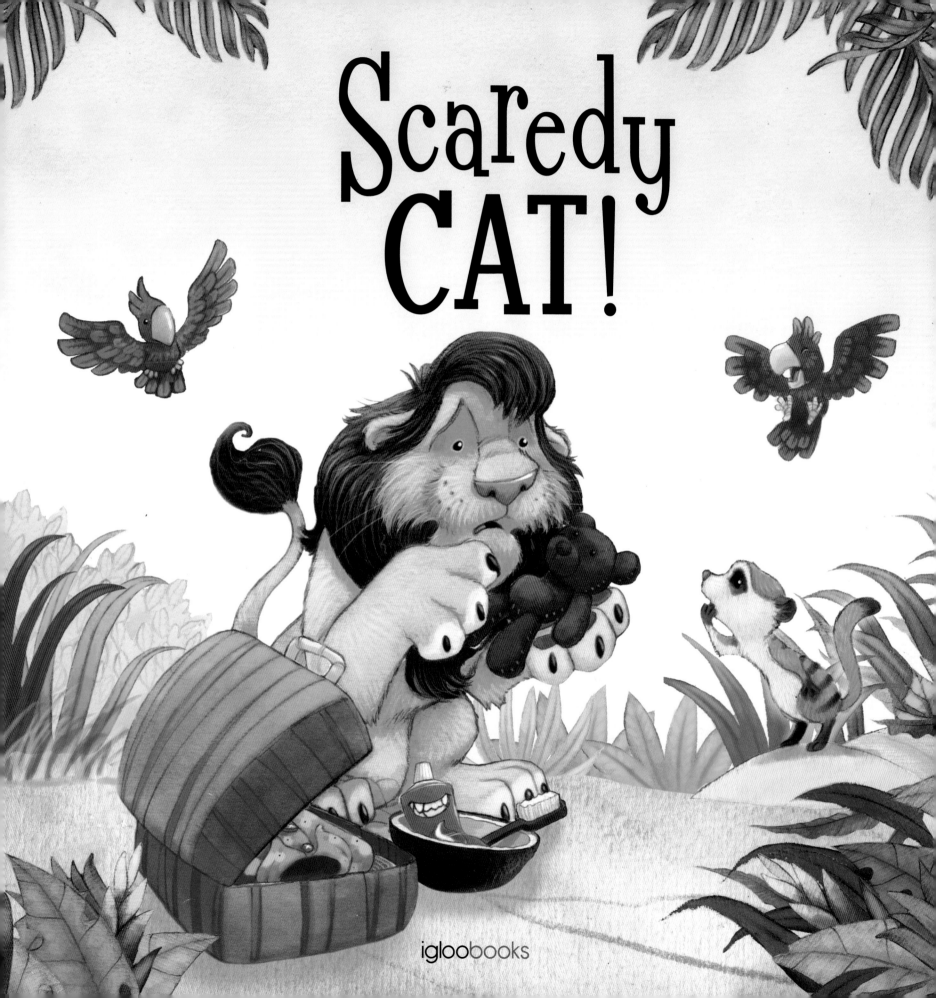

Scaredy CAT!

igloobooks

Once there was a lion
who was just **too** scared to roar.

When he tried...

... the monkeys howled...

... and rolled around the floor.

The lion **croaked**... ... and **grunted**.

He made such a **screeching** sound.

The parrots fell out of the trees and dived down underground.

"I'll **never** be king of the jungle," said Lion, feeling very sad.
"Cheer up," said a little meerkat. "Things really aren't that bad."

"Look at your reflection," said Meerkat.
"You're handsome and you're proud."

"Don't be scared of who you are. You should celebrate it out loud."

"Dry your eyes and cheer up, there's no need for you to cry.
We don't always get things right, the first time that we try."

So, Lion had another go.

He tried... ... and **tried**... ... and **tried.**

The monkeys found it hilarious and **laughed** until they cried.

"It's no use," said Lion, as he wiped away a tear.
"I'll pack my case and go. There's no place for me here."

"Please don't go," said Meerkat.
"There are more things we can try."

The monkeys **giggled** cheekily,
oo-ooed and said, "Goodbye."

The jungle animals wondered where their lion friend had gone.

"He's left the jungle," said the monkeys, "because he didn't belong."

"Someone has upset him," said Elephant.

"I want to find out who."

He waved his trunk at the monkeys.

"I suspect it's YOU."

"It's Meerkat's fault," cried the monkeys. "**He** drove Lion away!"

"Well, Meerkat?" asked Elephant, sternly. "What have **YOU** got to say?"

Poor Meerkat felt really silly, as everyone crowded round.
He shrunk back under the trees and crouched down on the ground.

"I want Lion to be **happy**," said Meerkat.

"To be the best that he can be.

I didn't want him to pack up and go.

Please don't pick on me."

Suddenly, there was a rustling.

A **flash** of a tail, then a paw.

Lion leapt out of the bushes and gave a **great big . . .**

"Leave him alone," said Lion and everyone stood and stared.
"You've found your roar!" **trumpeted** Elephant.
"Lion, you're not scared!"

OAR!

Everyone **cheered** for Lion.
The monkeys joined in, too.

"We're sorry," they said to Lion,
"that we were **mean** to you."

The animals had a party.
Lion was **much** happier than before.

"Thank you," he said to Meerkat,
"for helping me to find my **roar**."